The Treasure Hunt

by Audrey Tarrant

THE MEDICI SOCIETY LTD

LONDON

1986

THE TREASURE HUNT

'Atishoo! Atishoo!'

Skipton Tiptoes, the squirrel who lived in Town Park, had a bad cold.

'A-A-A-ATISHOO!'

'Oh dear me!' said Mrs Tiptoes, 'you need some good country air to blow those germs away. I think I will phone Aunt Cobnut in Talloaks, and ask her if you may go and stay with her for a few days.'

Skipton's friend Prickles Perkins, the hedgehog, had a bad cough, so Aunt Cobnut invited him also to Talloaks with Skipton.

The next day, Mrs Tiptoes took Skipton and Prickles to the station. Mr Hoppity the guard said he would look after them in the guard's van.

'Now lads, all luggage must have a label,' he laughed as he tied one round Skipton's neck. When he tried to tie one round Prickles' neck, he cried 'Ouch!' – and sucked his paw! Then, with a red pencil, he wrote on the label:-
    'HANDLE WITH CARE!'

Mr Hoppity blew the whistle and they were off. Chug-chug, chuggety-chug, chattered the train as it huffed and puffed its way slowly towards Talloaks.

'Would you like a biscuit, Mr Hoppity?' asked Skipton.

'Have one of mine, too,' said Prickles.

'Thankyou, that's very kind of you both,' said Mr Hoppity, as they finished their biscuits. 'Now, would you like to blow my whistle?'

Mr Hoppity carefully shut the windows so that no one could hear them.

'Pheep-pheep, PHEEP-PHEEP!'

Aunt Cobnut and Cousin Katie were waiting for them on Talloaks platform. As they walked home to Hazel Cottage, Skipton said, 'How quiet it is.'

'No cars, no buses,' said Prickles.

Suddenly there was a loud 'Karrk–karrk' from the bracken, and Skipton and Prickles jumped high in the air.

'Whatever was that dreadful noise?' gasped Skipton.

'It was only a pheasant,' laughed Katie. 'Haven't you heard one before?'

'N–no!' said Prickles thankfully, 'pheasants don't like living in Town Park.'

Soon Skipton and Prickles were used to the different country noises, and hopped and skipped happily down the narrow woodland paths with Katie.

One day Katie said, 'Let's go and pick blackberries'. Skipton and Prickles had never seen blackberries before, because the gardener did not like brambles growing in Town Park. Soon the basket was full.

'Let's see what the time is,' said Katie.

'How?' asked Prickles.

Katie pointed to the dandelion clock (the gardener allowed no dandelions to grow in Town Park).

They blew and blew – twelve puffs – 'so it's 12 o'clock, lunchtime!'

The next day they were very excited because it was the day for the Talloaks Treasure Hunt. All the young woodland animals went to Toadstool Corner where the trail started. Miss Mole rang the bell, and they were away. Katie, Skipton and Prickles scampered down the path, following the arrows of scarlet rosehips. Uphill and downhill, they ran so quickly that soon they were ahead of all the other animals.

They came to an arrow pointing across a
stream, where Mr Otter and Mr Water
Vole were waiting to row them over.
Skipton looked at the rocking boat, and
then up at the trees which stretched their
branches above the stream.

'I would rather jump across on those
branches,' he said.

'So would I,' said Katie.

Prickles watched Skipton cross, shiver-
ed, and then said firmly, 'Please, Mr Otter
and Mr Water Vole, *I* would much rather
go across in your boat.'

They ran down one path – and then another. They turned first to the left and then to the right.

'I can't see a red arrow anywhere,' said Skipton, just as Grandma Hare came along.

'Oh dear me!' she said, 'you seem to have lost the trail. I expect the wind has covered the arrow in the Dell with leaves. I must hurry along and uncover it for the other animals. You take the short cut after that silver birch and you will be back on the right path.'

'Oh, thank you!' they cried, as they scurried off. Soon they found the red arrows again, and they raced once more along the path. One, two, three – JUMP . . . Katie was over a fallen tree.

There was a screech and a squawk as she landed, to her great surprise, on a pheasant's tail. 'I'm sorry!' she gasped, but, muttering crossly, the pheasant flew away . . . leaving a long tail-feather behind.

Prickles picked it up, and stood to attention. 'Do you like my spear?' he asked, and they all laughed.

The last arrow, a bigger one, pointed towards a hollow oak tree. The Treasure must be inside it! They looked high and low, under the leaves and behind the cobwebs, but there was no treasure.

As they came out of the tree, there was a sudden gust of wind and a wild flurry of leaves. Prickles could not see where he was going; he stumbled, tripped over a tree-root and, curled in a ball, rolled down the bank into a ditch.

He picked himself up and began to climb the bank at the back of the oak tree. As he climbed he heard harsh voices and, looking over the top, he saw two naughty magpies pulling dried grass out of the roof of a dormouse's house, and banging on the door.

With leaves stuck to all his spines, and the pheasant's feather still in his hand, Prickles suddenly stood up and made himself visible . . . .

The magpies looked at him in horror – whatever was this THING with its rustling, flapping coat, its bright black eyes and its long spear? Screeching with fright, they flew away. Prickles walked towards the door, and then he saw it – yes, it really was – a bunch of hips hanging over the knocker! Squeaking with excitement, he called Skipton and Katie. They had found the Treasure!

Katie knocked on the door; it was opened at once and Mr and Mrs Dormouse asked them in. There on the table was the Treasure tied up in a large box. They untied the string and opened the box. Inside was another box tied up with string, and inside that another . . . . . and another . . . . . and another . . . . . until at last there it was . . . . . a bag of gold coins!

'Chocolate coins!' cried Katie.

'Scrumptious!' said Skipton as he rubbed his tummy.

'Mmmmm!' sighed Prickles happily.

Mr Dormouse went to tell the other animals that the Treasure had been found, and Mrs Dormouse said to the three friends, 'Thank you very much for frightening away those naughty magpies. We are having a firework party tonight, and you must come too.'

What a wonderful party it was!

SHOOOSH WHIRR BANG!

The fireworks burst in the air with all the colours of the rainbow. There were rockets and catherine wheels – and lots of sparklers.

After the fireworks, they went inside and had hot drinks, sandwiches and sticky buns. As Mr Dormouse filled the mugs, Skipton's tail tickled his nose and –
        'ATISHOO!'
    Mr Dormouse sneezed.
    Skipton and Prickles looked at each other – THEIR COLDS HAD GONE!

 B9 ISBN 0 85503 090 9